HONDA

The Boy Who Dreamed of Cars

by MARK WESTON • illustrated by KATIE YAMASAKI

LEE & LOW BOOKS INC. *New York*

Acknowledgments

I am indebted to three people. Louise May, Lee & Low's editor-in-chief, taught me how to turn a good story into a children's book. David Iida, Assistant to the President, Public Relations, Honda North America, Inc., gave advice about fine points in the text and was an enormous help with the illustrations. And my sister, Carol Weston, was a thoughtful editor and a wellspring of encouragement.—M.W.

Thank you to David Iida of Honda North America, Inc., who helped arrange my trip to Japan; and Keiko Seki, Customer Service Technology Development Division, Honda Motor Co., Ltd., for being a wonderful host, tour guide, and friend. Thank you for making my first trip to Japan such a joy. I am also grateful to my studio mates Yuko Shimizu and Marcos Chin for their constant support and friendship.—K.Y.

Author's Sources

Cameron, Kevin. "Soichiro's Ladder: Twenty-five years of technical progress." *Cycle,* September 1985: 60–80.

Gelsanliter, David. *Jump Start: Japan Comes to the Heartland.* Tokyo and New York: Kodansha, 1992.

Gibney, Frank. *Miracle by Design: The Real Reason Behind Japan's Economic Success.* New York: Times Books, 1982.

Gregory, Fred M. H. "What Makes Honda Run?" *Town and Country,* March 1985: 78–90.

Honda Motor Co., Ltd. Web site: http://honda.com

Kamioka, Kazuyoshi. *Japanese Business Pioneers.* Union City, CA: Heian International, 1988.

Mair, Andrew. *Honda's Global Local Corporation.* London and New York: St. Martin's, 1994.

Miller, Karen Lowry. "A Car is Born." *Business Week,* September 13, 1993: 64–72.

Mito, Setsuo. *The Honda Book of Management: A Leadership Philosophy for High Industrial Success.* London and Atlantic Highlands, NJ: Athlone Press, 1990.

Sakiya, Tetsuo. *Honda Motor: The Men, the Management, and the Machines.* Tokyo and New York: Kodansha, 1987.

Sanders, Sol W. *Honda: The Man and His Machine.* Boston: Little, Brown, 1975.

Schapp, John B. "Tycoon-San: The iconoclastic philosophy of Soichiro Honda." *Car and Driver,* June 1982: 28–29.

Shook, Robert L. *Honda: An American Success Story.* New York: Prentice Hall, 1988.

Stokes, Henry Scott. "Market Guzzler." *Fortune,* February 20, 1984: 105–108.

The NHK Group. *Good Mileage: The High-Performance Business Philosophy of Soichiro Honda.* Tokyo: NHK Publishing, 1996.

Troy, Stewart. "The Americanization of Honda." *Business Week,* April 25, 1988: 90–96.

Numerous articles from *The New York Times* and *The Wall Street Journal,* and some from *The Washington Post,* for current information about the Honda Motor Company and its products.

To my sister, Carol Weston, who also writes for children. Her help, from the first idea to the final draft, was invaluable.—M.W.

For Leo and Diane Dillon with so much love and gratitude—K.Y.

Text copyright © 2008 by Mark Weston
Illustrations copyright © 2008 by Katie Yamasaki
LEE & LOW BOOKS Inc., 95 Madison Avenue, New York, NY 10016
leeandlow.com
Manufactured in China
Book design by Christy Hale
Book production by The Kids at Our House
The text is set in Octavian
The illustrations are rendered in acrylic on canvas
10 9 8 7 6 5 4 3 2 1
First Edition
Library of Congress Cataloging-in-Publication Data
Weston, Mark.
Honda: the boy who dreamed of cars / by Mark Weston ; illustrated by Katie Yamasaki.
p. cm.
Summary: "A biography of Japanese businessman Soichiro Honda, founder of the Honda Motor Company, focusing on his early influences and later career as an innovative inventor and manufacturer of motorcycles and cars"—Provided by publisher.
ISBN 978-1-60060-246-7
1. Honda, Soichiro, 1906-1991. 2. Honda Giken Kogyo Kabushiki Kaisha—Biography.
3. Automobile industry and trade—Japan. 4. Executives—Japan—Biography.
5. Businesspeople—Japan—Biography. I. Yamasaki, Katie. II Title.
HD9710.J32H669 2008
338.7'6292092—dc22
[B]   2007049040

In the small Japanese town of Tenryu, far below snow-capped Mount Fuji, Soichiro Honda was born on November 17, 1906. As a boy he loved to watch the boats in the town's harbor. He wondered how the boats worked and where they went, and he dreamed of ports beyond the horizon.

Soichiro's mother wove cloth. His father worked as a blacksmith, hammering molten iron into fishing hooks, shovels, and farming tools. The oldest of nine children, Soichiro liked to watch his father make these things. He also helped his father chop big slabs of charcoal to stoke the fire in the blacksmith shop. The work was messy, and Soichiro was often covered with black charcoal dust.

One day when Soichiro was seven, a man drove a rumbling Ford Model T through town. Soichiro had never seen a car before. He ran beside it, amazed by the many moving parts. When he could run no farther, Soichiro crouched down and smeared his hands in a puddle of oil the car had left behind. He liked the smell. *Someday I will learn how a car works and make one myself,* he thought.

Soichiro was not a good student. Book learning did not make sense to him, but machinery did. When he was fifteen Soichiro moved to Tokyo, Japan's largest city. He found work in a garage where the owner, a mechanic, repaired American-made cars.

At first the garage owner was harsh. "Don't touch the cars, Soichiro," he said. "Your job is to sweep my garage and clean the tools. Nothing else. Do NOT touch the cars!"

Soichiro almost quit. "I want to learn how cars work," he muttered to himself.
"I didn't come to this big city just to sweep a floor." But he decided to stay. He
thought that if he kept the garage spotless, maybe the owner would be impressed
and teach him to be a mechanic.

Day after day Soichiro swept the garage and cleaned the tools. He worked hard and did not complain. After he finished his assigned duties, Soichiro watched the garage owner work. When the mechanic let him, Soichiro handed the man the tools he needed while he repaired the cars.

The garage owner noticed Soichiro's dedication. After almost a year he finally told the boy he was a good worker. "Now I will show you how to make some basic repairs," he said.

Soichiro was thrilled. *"Domo arigato gozaimasu,"* he said, bowing low. "Thank you very much."

For six years Soichiro trained as a mechanic. He learned how to fix every part of a car. He rebuilt carburetors, which mix air with gasoline, and he replaced the spark plugs that ignite this combustible mixture to power the engine and get a car going. He adjusted brakes, patched tires, and put in new water pumps. He even fixed transmissions, the gears that turn cars' wheels and allow cars to speed up and slow down.

Soichiro was now an expert repairman, and he wanted to run his own shop. Tokyo already had many mechanics, so Soichiro moved to Hamamatsu, a city near his hometown.

It was a proud day for Soichiro Honda when he opened his garage in 1928. He quickly became known as the best auto mechanic around, and the men in his shop repaired nearly every car in town. Within three years Honda had fifty employees working at his garage.

By the time he was in his late twenties, Honda had made a lot of money from his successful garage. He bought a house and married a schoolteacher named Sachi. Soon they began to raise a family.

In his spare time Honda started designing race cars. He loved to drive fast,

and in 1936 he built and drove the fastest race car in Japan. No sooner had Honda become the country's racing champion than he was seriously hurt in an accident. One of his brothers was also injured.

Honda's wife persuaded him to stop racing, but he still dreamed of making cars.

A year later Honda took an important step toward making his dream come true. He began manufacturing the metal rings that surround pistons. These small steel cups in a car's engine move up and down quickly inside cylinders as they convert the energy in gasoline into the force that turns a car's wheels.

Honda thought it would be easy to make piston rings, but his first ones were

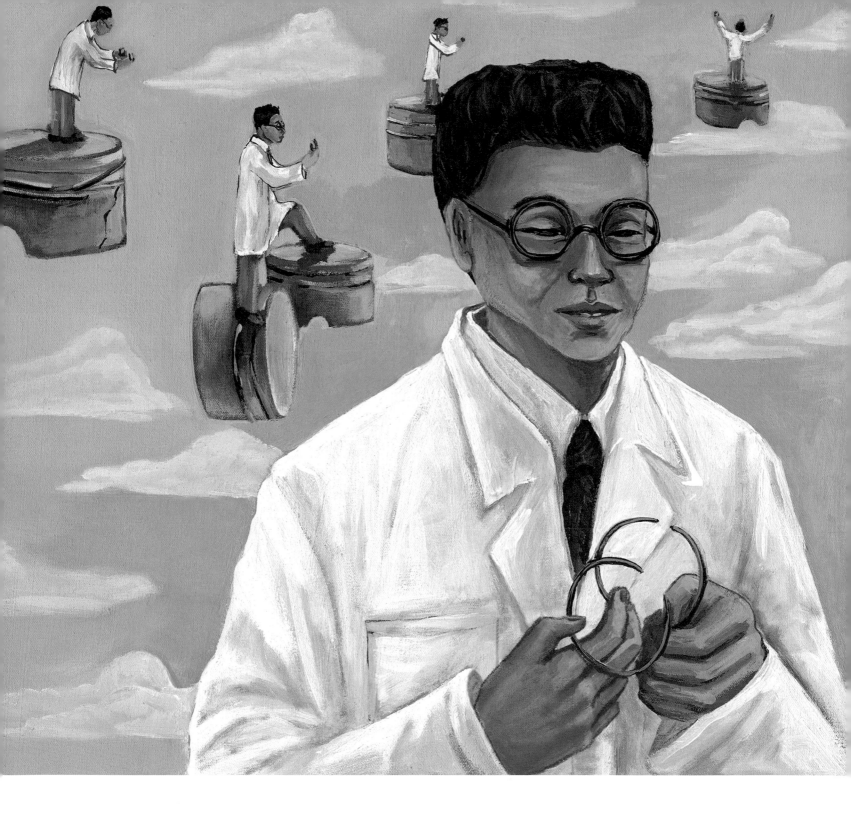

too rigid. They did not bend, and they cracked under stress. Ring after ring broke.
So Honda went back to school to study metallurgy, the science of working with
metal. Determined to figure out how to make his piston rings more flexible, Honda
tried one technical approach after another. By 1940 his piston rings worked perfectly.
He sold them to Toyota, one of Japan's first car companies.

In the early 1940s, during World War II, the Japanese air force asked Honda to make airplane propellers in addition to piston rings. When the war ended in 1945, Honda's propellers were no longer needed. Japan had been defeated. People could not afford to buy new cars, and car manufacturers did not need piston rings. Honda was discouraged, but he was able to make a living repairing old cars.

Gasoline was expensive after the war, so instead of driving to work, Honda often rode the train. He quickly grew tired of the crowded conditions, but the alternative—a bicycle—was too slow. Honda thought he could develop a faster bicycle. He added a tiny engine and a second chain belt, and turned a bicycle into a small motorcycle.

Honda converted five hundred bicycles into low-cost motorcycles. A local businessman, Takeo Fujisawa, was so impressed with these new machines that he raised money to build a motorcycle factory. Together, the two men started the Honda Motor Company. Fujisawa liked Honda's down-to-earth personality and did not mind when Honda wore work clothes to business meetings. Honda appreciated Fujisawa's skills as a salesman and his ability to secure loans from banks when the company needed to borrow money.

Honda eagerly kept up with the latest motorcycle technology because he wanted his motorcycles to be better than anyone else's. He figured out a way to double the power and gasoline mileage of his engines without making them more expensive. The small engines opened and shut like clamshells, which made it easy to reach the parts inside to make repairs.

Honda wanted all the motorcycles he made to be perfect. He often worked beside his employees on assembly lines and yelled at them when they made mistakes. "We are not selling clothes. We are selling motorcycles," Honda would shout. "If we don't tighten a nut properly, we put the customer's life in danger." The factory workers started calling him Mr. Thunder, and they worked hard because they did not want to displease him.

Although Honda had a temper, he treated his employees fairly. He offered good salaries, and built company gyms and swimming pools. Honda called his workers "associates." He encouraged them to share their ideas, and let them keep the money their inventions earned. Honda explained, "I have always had a stronger interest in the work than the money." He also created new jobs for associates when machines made their old jobs unnecessary.

By the late 1950s one third of Asia's motorcycles were Hondas. Now Honda had a new market to conquer. In 1959 the Honda Motor Company introduced its Super Cub motorcycles to the United States. Until then most Americans associated motorcycles with danger, loud noise, and gangs. But the Super Cub was too small

to be scary. The advertising slogan, You Meet the Nicest People on a Honda, projected an image of good, clean fun.

Sales soared as Americans who had never thought of riding motorcycles began buying them. Within five years the Honda Motor Company was making almost half of America's motorcycles.

In 1963 Honda returned to his lifelong dream of manufacturing cars. "I am not satisfied with being number one only in the motorcycle world," he told his associates. "Progress is when you go forward, when you keep graduating from one stage to another."

For six years Honda made small cars just for Japan. Then in 1969 he decided to start

shipping midsized cars to the United States. Before he did that he had to make a choice. Should the new cars have air-cooled or water-cooled engines? Honda admired the German air-cooled Volkswagens. After much thought, he decided that his engines would be air-cooled too. "Who wants pumps and hoses and things that leak?" he said.

Tadashi Kume, a young engineer, was convinced that Honda's decision was a mistake. Kume felt nervous about disagreeing with his boss, but he knew it was important to be honest. "Water-cooled engines are quieter and more powerful," he told Honda. "If you want to build bigger cars in the future, you will have to switch to water-cooled engines."

Honda encouraged his associates to speak their minds, and he realized that Kume was right. Honda reversed his decision. The water-cooled engine Kume helped design had better gas mileage and cleaner exhaust than other engines. It had a long name: the Compound Vortex Controlled Combustion engine. Its initials, CVCC, inspired the name of the first Honda car sold throughout the United States, the Civic.

The Honda Civic arrived in the United States in 1972. The timing was just right. Civics were the first cars to meet the stricter emissions standards of the Clean Air Act passed by Congress. When the price of gasoline quadrupled in 1973, Americans

started looking for cars that made better use of the expensive gas. On highways Honda Civics got forty-four miles per gallon, more than twice the mileage of most American cars. Sales of Honda cars in the United States skyrocketed.

In 1973, when Honda was sixty-six, he retired as president of the Honda Motor Company. He thought the company would stay creative if younger executives were in charge.

Honda remained a director of the company for many years but also took time to enjoy his retirement. He especially liked hang gliding, playing golf, painting,

and watching television on a set he installed in his bedroom ceiling. He died on August 5, 1991, at the age of eighty-four.

Many people today may never have heard of Soichiro Honda, but almost everyone knows his last name.

SOICHIRO HONDA

AP/WIDE WORLD PHOTOS

was an inventor with a passion for new ideas and improvements. He believed in the power of dreams and labored tirelessly to make his own dream of building cars come true. He worked, ate, and brainstormed with his employees, and saw failures as just necessary steps to success. Because he broke with tradition and preferred new ways of doing things, Soichiro Honda is regarded as one of the world's pioneering businessmen.

In 1982 the Honda Motor Company opened the first Japanese car factory in

the United States, in Marysville, Ohio. At first many Americans were not happy that a foreign-owned car factory had been built in their country. In protest, some people slashed the tires of Honda cars. As the company opened more plants, bringing good jobs and money to economically struggling towns and cities, Americans changed their minds. People in several areas of the country are now interested

in having Honda build plants in their communities.

Soichiro Honda left the world a unique manufacturing empire. As of 2008 the Honda Motor Company was selling about ten thousand cars a day worldwide—more than 3.6 million a year—and nearly four times as many motorcycles. Among its vast range of products, the company makes hybrid cars that help protect the environment because they run on electricity as well as gasoline, and small jets that operate as air taxis.

Today, Honda vehicles are everywhere, meeting the needs of consumers around the world. The popular cars and motorcycles are daily tributes to the work of a determined man who even as a boy dreamed of making his own cars.